Timo's Party

Victoria Allenby
Illustrated by **Dean Griffiths**

First published in the United States in 2017
First published in Canada in 2016

Text copyright © 2016 Victoria Allenby
Illustration copyright © 2016 Dean Griffiths
This edition copyright © 2016 Pajama Press Inc.
This is a first edition.
10 9 8 7 6 5 4 3 2 1

www.pajamapress.ca   info@pajamapress.ca

 Canada Council   Conseil des arts
for the Arts   du Canada
 ONTARIO ARTS COUNCIL
CONSEIL DES ARTS DE L'ONTARIO
an Ontario government agency
un organisme du gouvernement de l'Ontario
 Canadä

The publisher gratefully acknowledges the support of the Canada Council for the Arts and the Ontario Arts Council for its publishing program. We acknowledge the financial support of the Government of Canada through the Canada Book Fund (CBF) for our publishing activities.

Library and Archives Canada Cataloguing in Publication

Allenby, Victoria, 1989-, author

    Timo's party / Victoria Allenby ; illustrated by Dean Griffiths.

ISBN 978-1-77278-008-6 (hardback)

    I. Griffiths, Dean, 1967-, illustrator II. Title.

PS8601.L44658T57 2016   jC813'.6   C2016-903199-3

Publisher Cataloging-in-Publication Data (U.S.)

Names: Allenby, Victoria, 1989-, author. | Griffiths, Dean, 1967-, illustrator.
Title: Timo's party / Victoria Allenby ; illustrated by Dean Griffiths.
Description: Toronto, Ontario Canada : Pajama Press, 2016. | Summary: "Timo struggles with his dislike for big parties when his friend Hedgewick asks him to host an apple festival in his orchard. Knowing the festival will help bring Hedgewick's cooking to the attention of an important food critic, Timo resolves to help his friend, and learns more about his own strengths along the way"— Provided by publisher.
Identifiers: ISBN 978-1-77278-008-6 (hardcover)
Subjects: LCSH: Parties – Juvenile fiction. | Rabbits – Juvenile fiction. | Friendship -- Juvenile fiction. | BISAC: JUVENILE FICTION / Readers / Intermediate. | JUVENILE FICTION / Social Themes / Friendship. | JUVENILE FICTION / Animals / Rabbits.
Classification: LCC PZ7.S658Lit |DDC [E] – dc23

Cover and book design—Rebecca Bender

Manufactured by Qualibre Inc./Printplus
Printed in China

Pajama Press Inc.
181 Carlaw Ave. Suite 207 Toronto, Ontario Canada, M4M 2S1

Distributed in Canada by UTP Distribution
5201 Dufferin Street Toronto, Ontario Canada, M3H 5T8

Distributed in the U.S. by Ingram Publisher Services
1 Ingram Blvd. La Vergne, TN 37086, USA

For Megan
—V.A.

To Steve,
Supreme Allied
Cookmander
—D.G.

Chapter One

Timo loved the fall. He loved the warm sun and the cool breeze, the taste of rain and the smell of leaves.

Most of all, Timo loved picking apples in the orchard behind his home—as long as he did not have to climb a ladder to reach them.

On the first day of harvest, Timo kept his paws safely on the ground while he picked the low-hanging fruit. The orchard was as quiet as a wish. The sun beamed. The leaves rustled. The apples gleamed—and then someone bustled around the corner of the house.

"Timo!" Hedgewick hurried across the grass, waving a newspaper. His spikes shook and his eyes shone. "Look at this!"

Timo took the newspaper. While Hedgewick hopped from paw to paw, Timo read:

FAMOUS FOOD CRITIC TO VISIT TOADSTOOL CORNERS

BY PADMA LILI, NEWS REPORTER

Chip and Chuck Wood, owners of The Burrow Inn, report that the well-known travel writer and food critic Madame LaPointe will be coming to stay this weekend. She is writing a series of articles about the best small towns to visit. Mayor Lin Song says, "I know everyone in town will work hard to show Madame LaPointe the very best of Toadstool Corners."

"Madame LaPointe," said Timo. "Is she that porcupine who visits restaurants and writes about them in newspapers?"

"Yes," said Hedgewick, "And she is the one who discovered Bruno Grizzle. He is a famous baker now."

Timo knew that Hedgewick dreamed of being a famous chef. "Are you hoping she will discover you?"

"Oh! Oh, no. I am not good enough yet." Hedgewick looked down at his paws.

"Of course you are," said Timo. "When you cooked for Ratna Chitter's birthday party, the mayor said you were the best chef in town."

Hedgewick blushed. "That was kind of her. I guess it is too bad there are no birthday parties to cook for this weekend."

"Hmm." Timo tugged an ear, thinking. "Maybe someone can throw another kind of party."

"A party for what?"

"A party for..." Timo did not have an answer. He scrunched his forehead. He scratched his fur. Then he looked at the apple in his paw. "For apples?"

Hedgewick stared at Timo. Then his snout wrinkled and his eyes crinkled. His smile was as wide as the sky. "An apple festival!" he said. "Apple pie. Apple dumplings. Bobbing for apples. Oh, Timo! Will you really do that for me?"

"Will I—will I what?" said Timo.

"Host an apple festival in your orchard! It is such a good idea. The whole town can come!"

"Oh!" said Timo. "Y-yes. Of course."

"Thank you! Thank you!" Hedgewick scurried off to plan his menu.

Timo hurried into his house and shut the door.

Oh, no, he thought. *Oh, no, no, no.*

Chapter Two

Timo was not a shy rabbit. Not exactly.

He could stand on stage and give a speech. He could shake a stranger's paw. He could make his friends laugh.

But big parties made his fur stand on end.

Whenever Timo was in a crowd, his head would ache. His knees would quake. And he could never, ever think of anything to say.

"How can I host a big party if I cannot even talk to anyone?" he cried. "I cannot do it. I do not want to do it."

But the party was important to Hedgewick. Timo did want to help his friend.

"I know what will make me feel better," he said. "A list."

Timo fetched his notebook. He wrote:

Things I need for the party

- Invitations
- Decorations
- Games

"That is not so bad," he said. "I only need to do three things. No problem." He started right away.

Madame LaPointe, guest
The Burrow Inn
Toadstool Corners

Dear Madame LaPointe,

You are invited to the
Toadstool Corners Apple Festival!

Where: Timo's Orchard, 33 Meadow Lane
When: Saturday at 4 p.m.
What: Good fun and good food
prepared by Hedgewick Stump

We hope to see you there!

Sincerely,

Timo Vega

Timo wrote the address on an
envelope and slipped the letter inside.

"There," he said. "Now I just have to
make one for everyone in town."

With a twitch of his whiskers, Timo
got to work. He wrote invitations until
the sun went down.

Chapter Three

In the morning, Timo knocked on Hedgewick's door.

"I am in the kitchen!" Hedgewick called.

The counter was covered in papers. The floor was buried in books. Hedgewick sat on a stack of recipe cards.

"Hello!" he said. "I am planning my menu."

"I brought you a party invitation," said

Timo. "I have written one for everyone in town."

Hedgewick smiled. "You are so organized. That is why you will be such a good host for this party."

Timo did not want to think about that.

"I have to go deliver the invitations," he said.

The stacks of envelopes slipped and slid in Timo's wagon as he started down the road. Just then, Suki came over the hill.

"Hello, Timo!" she said. "What are all these letters for?"

"They are invitations," said Timo. "I promised Hedgewick I would host a party."

Suki laughed. "You? But you hate parties."

"I know. But Hedgewick wants to

impress Madame LaPointe with his cooking. It is his dream. How could I say no?"

Suki ruffled Timo's ears. "You are a good friend. I will help you deliver the invitations."

"Thank you," said Timo. "I am glad to be a good friend, but I do not think I will be a very good host."

"That is easy," said Suki. "You just have to be more confident. Stand up tall. Taller. No, do not let your ears lie flat."

Timo tried. He stood as tall as a pine tree. He imagined his ears tickling the sky.

"Good!" Suki clapped him hard on the back.

Timo flinched. His ears flopped. "I do not think standing tall will make me braver," he said.

"It will make you *look* brave," said Suki. "That is the first step."

After the invitations were delivered, Timo went back to his orchard. Hedgewick would need a lot of apples for all those recipes. With a flick of his ears, Timo got to work. He picked apples until the sun went down.

Chapter Four

In the morning, Timo carried a basket of apples to Hedgewick's house. He knocked on the door.

"I am in the kitchen!" called Hedgewick.

The kitchen looked like it had been in a blizzard. White flour floated in the air. It coated the counter. It settled on the stove.

"Hello!" said Hedgewick. "I am making pastry today. We will need a lot of pies!"

"I cannot wait to taste them," said Timo. "I have brought some apples for you to use."

Hedgewick beamed. "Thank you. You are so generous. That is why you will be such a good host for this party."

Timo was not so sure about that. "I have to go make decorations," he said.

Timo found plenty of paint at the craft store. He also found rolls of ribbons, rows of bows, and glitter galore.

There is so much to choose from, thought Timo. Staring at it all, he almost walked into Rae.

"Hello, Timo!" said Rae. "Suki gave me an invitation from you."

"Yes," said Timo. "I am hosting a big party. That is why I am buying things to make decorations."

Rae looked worried. "But you hate parties."

"I know, but Hedgewick wants to cook for Madame LaPointe. I could not say no."

Rae patted Timo's paw. "You are a good friend. Can I help you make the decorations?"

Soon they were both sitting at Timo's kitchen table.

Timo wrote names on tags.

Rae painted apples on flags.

They pasted.

They basted.

Then Rae said, "You look unhappy."

"I am worried about the party," said Timo. "I do not think I will be a good

host. I will not know what to say to anyone."

"That is easy," said Rae. "You just ask questions about things that interest them."

"What if I cannot think of any questions?"

"We can practice now," said Rae. "Hello, Timo. This is a very nice party."

"Thank you, Rae. Ummm..." Timo frowned. What could he ask Rae? "Have you invented any new machines lately?"

"I am working on one," said Rae. "It is supposed to fold laundry, but so far it only ties it in knots." She smiled. "See? Now we are talking. That was not so hard."

"Hmm," said Timo.

When the decorations were finished, Rae went home. Timo went out to the orchard.

I will have to make everything tidy, he thought. There were fallen apples to pick up, leaves to rake up, and branches to gather up. Timo rolled up his sleeves and got down to work. He cleaned the orchard until the sun went down.

Chapter Five

On the morning of the party, Timo went to check on Hedgewick. He knocked on the door.

"I am in the kitchen!" Hedgewick called.

The kitchen looked like it had been in an earthquake. Everywhere Timo looked were piles of plates and lots of pots. One dish dripped with sauce. Another overflowed with oats. Quite a few were full of fruit.

Hedgewick was stirring something thick and sticky. "Hello!" he said. "I am so excited. Just look at all this food!"

"Yes," said Timo, looking around. "That is why I am here—to see if you need help getting everything ready in time."

"Oh, I do not need help," said Hedgewick, "But thank you for asking. You are so thoughtful. That is why you will be such a good host tonight."

Timo wished he were as confident as Hedgewick. "I will go start setting up, then," he said.

At home, Timo carried the decorations outside. He got out a tub for apple-bobbing, rings for ring-toss, and sacks for a sack race.

"I guess I will have to get out the ladder, too," Timo said. He did not like it, but there were banners to be hung and streamers to be strung.

Timo clung to the ladder with one paw and a banner with the other. He stretched.He strained. He reached. He—

Then the banner ripped, Timo

slipped, and the ladder tipped over with a **CRASH**.

"Maybe Hedgewick does not need help," said Timo, "but I do." Just then he saw Bogs coming through the meadow.

"I am so glad to see you!" cried Timo. "Are you here to help me set up?"

"Who, me?" said Bogs. He looked behind him, but there was no one else there. Then he looked at Timo in his tangle of decorations. One corner of his mouth turned up in a smile. "Oh, all right."

Bogs and Timo hung the decorations. They arranged tables and chairs. They set up the games.

After a while, Bogs said, "I thought you hated parties."

Timo moved a fork a little to the left. "I do. But I am hosting this one to help Hedgewick."

"I thought crowds made you nervous," said Bogs.

"They do," said Timo, re-folding a napkin. "But this may help Hedgewick become a famous chef. We have invited Madame LaPointe."

"I thought you were terrible at talking to strangers," said Bogs.

Timo's shoulders sagged. "I am. Rae and Suki have given me good advice, but it is not easy to follow."

"Oh, I can give you some easy advice," said Bogs. "Stand next to someone who likes to talk. Then you will only need to listen and nod."

"That is easy advice," Timo agreed. "But I think the host must talk to more than one person."

"That," said Bogs, "is why I never host parties."

Chapter Six

In the afternoon, Timo helped Hedgewick carry all the food to the orchard.

There was sweet apple bread and sour apple soup, hot apple cider and apple iced tea. There were plump apple dumplings and glazed apple pastries, and pies as far as the eye could see.

Hedgewick wiped his face. "I did not quite finish roasting my apple-nut-stuffed squash. May I use your kitchen?"

"My kitchen?" said Timo. "Oh. Of course."

While Hedgewick cooked, Timo went outside. He looked up the road. He looked down the road. It was empty.

"No one is coming," he said to himself. "Maybe no one will come at all."

Timo walked into the orchard. He walked out of the orchard. He walked back in and moved one chair a little to the right.

Maybe only our very best friends will come.

"What lovely decorations!" said a voice. "Am I the first to arrive?"

Timo spun around. The mayor of Toadstool Corners ruffled her feathers and smiled at him.

"Y-yes," said Timo. He took a deep breath. It was time to be a good host. He stood up as tall as a pine tree. He stretched his ears until they tickled the sky. "Welcome to the apple festival," he said. And then he blinked. He blanked.

What should he say next?

"Mrs. Mayor, how good to see you," said a new voice. Rae had arrived. She winked at Timo and asked the mayor, "How is your plan for the new bridge coming?"

Relieved, Timo turned away. A new guest was arriving. "Welcome to the apple festival, Mr. Totter," he said.

"Thank you, young rabbit," said the old turtle. He blinked slowly.

Timo thought fast. He should ask a question now—but what? He did not know Mr. Totter well. "Do—do you have any interests?" he squeaked.

"Any interests?" Mr. Totter repeated. "Well, I suppose I am fond of flies."

"Oh! Well," said Timo. He did not know much about flies, either. "Well, then, you should talk to my friend Bogs. He likes flies. There he is now. Goodbye!" Timo waved to Bogs, who was coming through the apple trees. Then he turned tail and ran into the house.

"Oh, Hedgewick," Timo moaned, leaning against the door. "I am *not* a good host. I hope you are ready to come serve the food. Hedgewick? Where are you?"

"I am in the kitchen." Hedgewick's voice was very quiet. Timo followed it, then stopped in shock.

The kitchen looked like it had been in a fire. The pans on the counter were as black as midnight. The squashes in the pans were as black as ink. The smoke above the squashes was as black as a nightmare.

"What happened?" he asked.

Hedgewick looked embarrassed. "I was daydreaming about what Madame LaPointe would say when she tasted my apple-nut-stuffed squash. I know what she would say now." He waved a paw at the burnt food. "She would say it is a disaster."

"There is plenty of other food," said Timo.

"But the squash was the main course.
The menu is not complete without it.
What will I do?"

Timo looked at the food. He looked
at his friend. He squared his shoulders.
"You will make a new main course," he
said, "and I will serve the food."

Outside, Timo picked up a tray.
He walked over to a group of guests.

"Please try a tart," he said. "My friend Hedgewick baked them with apples from this orchard."

"How interesting," said Padma.

"How tasty," said Nik.

When the tray was empty, Timo filled it with glasses. "Have you had any cider?" he asked. "My friend Hedgewick made it from an old family recipe."

"How wonderful," said Chip.

"How refreshing," said Chuck.

"May I try some, young rabbit?" asked a voice Timo did not know. He turned to see a porcupine carrying a notebook.

"Of course," he said. "You must be Madame LaPointe. Welcome to the apple festival." He remembered the newspaper article. "Have you had many interesting adventures visiting small towns?"

"Ah, yes," said Madame LaPointe, sipping her cider. "Let me tell you about the harvest fair in Song Hollow." Madame LaPointe talked. Timo listened and nodded. Then Hedgewick came out with a big, blue bowl.

"The main course tonight," he said, "is apple-nut spinach salad."

Everyone clapped.

"How simple," said Madame LaPointe. She wrote something down in her notebook. "I do like simple."

Chapter Seven

A few days after the festival, Timo's friends helped him pick the last apples. The orchard looked as empty as an echo with no apples, no decorations, and no party guests.

"Thank you for all your help," he said. "I could not have finished on my own."

"That is because you have been too busy helping me," said Hedgewick. "You were a great host."

"You did not look nervous at all," said Suki.

"And you talked with everyone," said Rae.

"It was easy to talk about Hedgewick's food," said Timo. "And it was easy when I had a job to do."

Just then, Bogs pulled something out of his pocket. "I suppose you want to see this," he said. "It was in today's newspaper."

It was Madame LaPointe's article. Hedgewick gasped. Suki grinned. Rae smoothed the crumpled paper.

FRESH FALL FUN IN TOADSTOOL CORNERS

BY MADAME L. LAPOINTE, FOOD CRITIC

Toadstool Corners is an excellent spot for any traveler seeking a meadow or riverside escape. The Burrow Inn is cozy and comfortable. The ice-cream shop is one of the best I have visited. Come in the fall to attend the Apple Festival, an event catered by up-and-coming chef Hedgewick Stump. Host Timo Vega is a charming party planner, and I am already looking forward to next year.

"Up-and-coming chef!" whispered Hedgewick, his spikes trembling with joy. "She called me an up-and-coming chef!"

But Timo was not listening. "Next year?" He whispered. "Oh, no. Oh, no, no, no."

HEDGEWICK'S HAPPY APPLE-BANANA CAKE

Ingredients

2–3 ripe bananas
3 eggs
1 cup applesauce
½ cup plain yogurt
1 teaspoon vanilla
3 tablespoons honey
2 ¾ cups flour
2 teaspoons baking powder
2 teaspoons salt
3 teaspoons cinnamon
2 teaspoons ground ginger
1 apple, peeled, cored, and chopped
¼ cup flour
1 tablespoon white sugar

Caution: You must have an adult assist you when you make this recipe—especially when using the oven.

Directions

1. Preheat the oven to 350° Fahrenheit.
2. Mash the bananas in a large bowl. Add the eggs and mix well. Stir in the applesauce, yogurt, vanilla, and honey.
3. In another bowl, mix the 2 ¾ cups flour, baking powder, salt, cinnamon, and ginger.
4. Stir together the wet and dry ingredients.
5. In a small bowl, mix the remaining flour with the sugar. Add the chopped apple and toss until coated.
6. Using a spatula, gently fold the coated apple pieces into the batter.
7. Grease two loaf pans with butter or oil. Spoon in the batter until the pans are three quarters full.
8. Bake until golden brown, or until a toothpick inserted in the middle comes out clean, about 1 hour.